JENNIFER'S RABBIT

Tom Paxton

Illustrated by Donna Ayers

Morrow Junior Books / New York

Library of Congress Cataloging-in-Publication Data
Paxton, Tom.
Jennifer's rabbit.
Summary: In a dream, Jennifer, a rabbit, a turtle,
a kangaroo, and seventeen monkeys visit the ocean with
the cookie-crumb sands.
[1. Dreams—Fiction.   2. Stories in rhyme]   I. Ayers,
Donna, ill.   II. Title.
PZ8.3.P2738Je 1988   [E]   87-14113
ISBN 0-688-07431-6
ISBN 0-688-07432-4 (lib. bdg.)

To Jennifer
—T.P.

To my mother
—D.A.

Jennifer slept in her little bed
With dreams of her rabbit in her little head.

Jennifer's rabbit, brown and white,
Left the house and ran away one night,

Along with a turtle and a kangaroo,
And seventeen monkeys from the city zoo…

And Jennifer, too.

They ran through the forest and they all held hands.

They came to the ocean with the cookie-crumb sands.
They called it the sea of the very best dreams,

And they all built a castle of the best moonbeams
And Milky Way streams.

And there on the sands where the starfish play,
The ship sailed in from the moonbeam bay.

They all went sailing on the starlight sea,
Where they all had cookies with oolong tea....
And Jenny had three.

They danced on the decks of the red-sailed brig.
The monkeys and the sailors did a whirling jig.
Turtle played the fiddle and the rabbit played kazoo,
And they bowed to each other as polite folks do....

And Jenny bowed, too.

Then, "My," said the turtle as the clock struck three,
"The hour is growing very late for me."
"Not at all," said the rabbit, "and I'll tell you why.
We still haven't counted every star in the sky...."

Said Jenny, "Let's try."

So they counted on the ship

and they counted on the shore.

They counted through the forest to the bedroom door.

They counted in bed till they could count no more.
Then they all fell asleep, and the final score
Was a trillion and four.

Yes, the rabbit and the turtle and the kangaroo,
And Jenny fell asleep as sleepy folk do,

Just like you....